A Tony Millionaire Sock Monkey Adventure

FOR Izzy

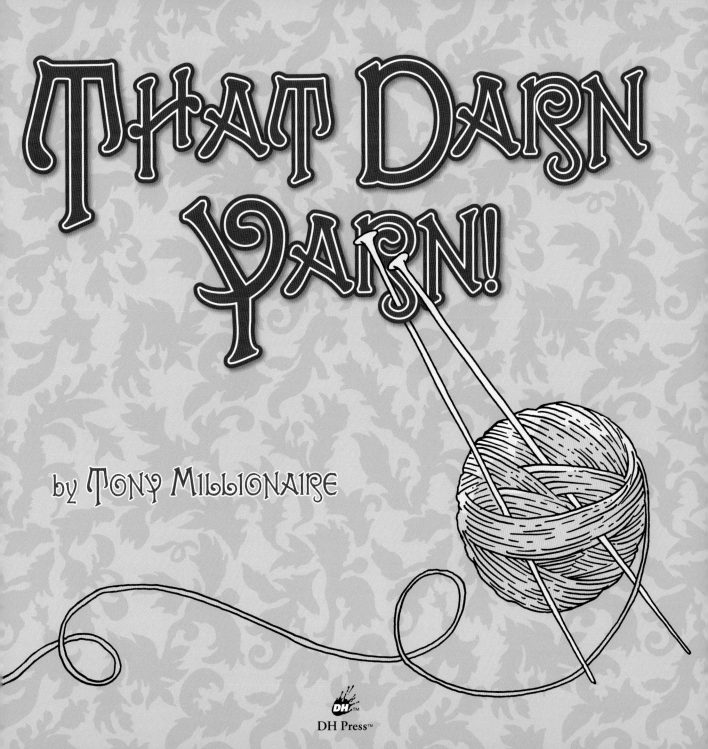

That Darn Yarn!

by Tony Millionaire

DH™

DH Press™

DESIGNER ··· LIA RIBACCHI

EDITOR ··· DAVE LAND

PUBLISHER ··· MIKE RICHARDSON

THAT DARN YARN!

DH Press™
A division of Dark Horse Comics, Inc.
10956 SE Main Street
Milwaukie, OR 97222

First edition: May 2005
ISBN: 1-59582-009-4

10 9 8 7 6 5 4 3 2 1
PRINTED IN CHINA